The Missing Peace

by
Kiffany Miller-Caldwell

Copyright Notice

Kiffany Miller-Caldwell
The Missing Peace

© 2014, Kiffany Caldwell
Anointed Fire™ Christian Book Publishing
kiffany.caldwell@yahoo.com

ISBN-13: 978-0692297865
ISBN-10: 0692297863

Dedication

I dedicate this book to the ONLY Wise GOD:
My Creator, my King, and my Father. Thanks
for trusting the heart of Your people to me.

Acknowledgments

I would like to thank my husband, JerMarlon Caldwell, for serving as my support in ministry. I love you honey. I would also like to thank my five children: LaKevia, Imani, JerMyra, JerMarlon II and Carson Chance for allowing me to steal away many nights to complete the first of a series of books that will be birthed. I will not leave out my mother, who has believed in me from the very start. Mother, I love you more every second. Just when I feel like I'm too weak to carry on, you carry me. I thank you. To my darling sisters: Tiffany, Kameka, and Taneka: You have all been more of a blessing than words can say, and I love you with a love that will never end. Thank you to my Uncle Leo who encouraged and assured me that writing, if done with passion, flows from the heart to each page in unison. To my Uncle Scott, thanks for being the best uncle a girl could ever ask for. I love you. To all of my family and friends, I love you and thank you for all of your prayers. They were my strength throughout this process. Thanks.

Table of Contents

Introduction

The Missing Peace was taken from Isaiah 26:3 KJV, which reads, "Thou wilt keep him in perfect peace, whose mind is stayed on thee: because he trusted in thee."

In The Missing Peace, you will find storms and challenges that the human race faces daily. In this book, the characters are just like each of us. We have all found ourselves in situations that made us feel betrayed, sad, angry, uncomfortable or ashamed. Each trial was a lesson learned. We have the victory, through Christ Jesus

Chapter 1

Broken Promises

Ring…. Ring… It was three o'clock in the morning at the Willis home.

"Who could possibly be calling at this time?" asked Granny Big. The old floor made creeping sounds as Granny Big made her way towards the telephone. This was not the first time that the phone had rung at three in the morning. For the last few weeks, calls in the middle of the night had become commonplace. By the time Granny Big answered the phone, there was nothing but silence on the line. It was like déjà vu .Worry clouded Granny Big's mind because Jazzy, her son's ex-girlfriend, was expected to deliver her triplets in less than a week. Granny Big did not approve of the youngsters having children out of wedlock.

Granny Big's family, as far as she could remember, believed in the bible, and to have her son, Cliff, act as if he did not know right from wrong caused her much shame.

Cliff did understand though. He went to church every Sunday and oftentimes attended bible study. He sang in the youth choir and played on the church's basketball team. He loved playing for the Fierce Warriors, and they loved him just as much. He believed the bible, or at least, he thought he did. When Cliff started college, he barely attended church until it was Christmas because the church always had a great raffle during the holidays. The winner of the raffle would win the latest electronic game and a fifty dollar gift card to the winner's favorite eatery. Cliff would also show up to church for Easter and sometimes for Mother's Day to make his mother happy.

Broken Promises

Jazzy (Cliff's ex-girlfriend) did not have family in Cover City. Jazzy was a freshman at Slydale Community College. SCC was one of the four schools that offered her an academic scholarship. She chose the community college to be near her mother. Her graduating class only had thirty-seven students in it. Jazzy maintained the highest grade average in every class she'd attended. She had her head on straight and vowed that she would not let anything take her away from her goals. Even after starting college, Jazzy would often spend countless nights at the library or attend work-study at the café on campus. To her, this was the life.

Colorful flyers advertising the big game set to take place that night were posted all around school. While at work, a student came through Jazzy's line to buy a sandwich and cappuccino, holding a flyer. Jazzy had never attended a high school game before and the thought of going to a college game was unreal.

The rain outside was drizzling and all Jazzy wanted to do was go to her dorm room and sleep. After a quick nap, she intended to study for her Nutrition class. She considered going to see what all this basketball hype was about, but after her tiring day at the café, she decided against it.

Jazzy drove back to her dorm room planning to take a shower, grab something to eat, and prepare her study materials before turning in for the night.

Walking up to her rooming quarters was relaxing. The lighting was dim and the sound of crickets chirping comforted her. When Jazzy opened her room's door, she saw her roommate, Mary, ironing a red shirt. Mary's curlers were lying on her bed. It was obvious that Mary had plans.

Mary: Jazzy, will you ride to the game with me? Please? Pretty please?

Jazzy: I'm not interested in going to the game. Besides, I really don't want to see a bunch of sweaty, funky thugs running over each other. I don't know what the big deal is about this game.

Mary: Jazzy, please go with me. If you don't have fun, I won't ask you to go again.

Jazzy: Okay, just this once.

At the game, Mary saw a group of girls that took psychology class with her. In the group was Mary's best friend, Tina. Mary introduced Jazzy to Tina and the rest of the group. It was finally time for the boys to play.

They came out wearing orange, white and

navy uniforms. The crowd was screaming because the boys' team was undefeated. The cheerleaders were cheering loudly and waving their pom-poms with excitement. The smell of popcorn and chili dogs made Jazzy hungry, but she wanted to see if the game was worth her time and attention before settling down to eat.

Suddenly, Jazzy saw player number 69, and boy was he fine. Jazzy wanted to ask someone who he was, but she was too shy to make it known that she was interested in him. Besides, she had never seen him around campus, plus, he was an athlete. It was a known fact that athletes were infamous for partying and having their way with as many girls as they could. She was not about to let her mind go there. Jazzy could not keep her eyes off of number 69. This beautiful specimen of a man was quite the athlete. He won the game with a thrilling three point shot at the sound of the buzzer.

Broken Promises

After the game, Mary decided to wait around for Beth, who was a cheerleader for the SCC Thunder. Jazzy was still hungry, so while waiting, she walked over to the concession stand to buy a bag of potato chips and a cold drink. To her surprise, player number 69 stood at the concession booth with his back turned to her. As she walked closer, the now unsuited basketball star was looking in her direction. Jazzy didn't feel hungry anymore. Just as she turned around to search for Mary, she heard a voice say, "Excuse me."

She acted as if she could not hear the gentlemen, using the noise in the hallway as her cover. The young man walked faster as Jazzy attempted to get away from him.

He kept saying, "Excuse me. Excuse me. Don't you work in the café on campus?"

Surprised, Jazzy turned around. "May I help you?

Cliff: Where are my manners? My name is Cliff Willis. What's your name, if I may ask?

Jazzy: Jazzy Dents is my name, but my friends call me Jazzy.

Cliff: I have seen you once or twice in the café and wondered if you ever hang out because I never see you around.

Jazzy: Well, I kind of stay to myself.

Cliff: May I have your number, Jazzy?

Jazzy: I'm sorry. I don't know enough about you to give you my number. How do I know if you aren't like the others?

Cliff: Why are you playing hard to get? I just want to be your friend.

Jazzy: I don't know about that.

The following day, Cliff walked into the café while Jazzy was at work and asked if he could buy her a sandwich on her lunch break. She took Cliff up on his offer. The couple sat in one of the booths and talked for Jazzy's entire break. Time seemed to fly by and the conversation was good.

Jazzy's curiosity was aroused and she definitely wanted to see Cliff again. She loved the way Cliff looked at her. She had never met anyone who made her feel as special as Cliff did, even though she was a little scared to give her heart to him.

Jazzy was a country girl from a small town called Joliet in Alabama. For the most part, everyone in Joliet knew each other, and the closeness of the community felt really good.

She had never had a boyfriend prior to Cliff. Her mother, Glenda, was an elementary school teacher and Jazzy did not know her father. All she knew about her father was that he was an alcoholic who never came around. Her mother once told her that when she was old enough to understand, she would tell her all that she wanted to know concerning her dad. Jazzy didn't think much about her dad growing up. She'd simply convinced herself that he did not exist.

Jazzy never had many friends from grade school to high school, but she longed to have someone that she could love. Out of six siblings, Jazzy was the black sheep of the family. Her brothers were much older and had families of their own, and her sisters had moved away to various parts of the country while she was in elementary. High school years were quite tough for the young teen, but somehow, someway, she had made it. Or had she?

Broken Promises

Jazzy often wondered how people around her appeared happy with their families. Jazzy had seen parents coming in and out of the café with their children where she worked, and each time she became extremely sad. Jazzy wished for the day that someone would care enough about her to show up and remain a constant presence in her life.

Cliff was a sophomore at SCC. Cliff, much like Jazzy, came to SCC on an athletic scholarship. Cliff often dreamed of playing basketball in the NBA. In fact, there were rumors that a scout would be coming to SCC the following month for possible draft picks.
Outside of sports, Cliff majored in art and loved to draw and express his emotions through art.

Finally, after her break was over, Jazzy gave Cliff the phone number to her dorm room and he gave Jazzy his cell number. She told him that she was a nursing student and that she would barely have time for anything except work study at the café and classes.

Every week thereafter, the newly found friends would meet on Thursdays to have lunch in the center court of the campus.

****

One Thursday evening, Jazzy and Cliff were at the café when Jazzy placed her hand on Cliff's shoulder. "Cliff, I am really enjoying the attention that you are giving me."

Cliff: I have never had anyone to give me as much attention and laughter as you have given me in the last few weeks either.

Jazzy: What are you going to do for me to celebrate our two month anniversary?

Cliff: Jazzy, I cannot tell you my plans because I don't want to blow my cover.

Broken Promises

Jazzy thought that it was romantic for Cliff to be making plans for their two month anniversary. Later that evening, Cliff called his friend, Lance, to get a little advice.

Cliff: Lance, what should I buy my girl, cause she talking about plans for this two month thing?

Lance: Mane, you shouldn't buy that chic nothing because you haven't known her long enough to be buying gifts.

Cliff: I am really feeling this young lady. I really enjoy our time together, and I don't want to disappoint her by not showing up with a gift or doing something.

Lance: Cliff, if you spend money on her, get what you want at least.

Cliff: No, man, I can't do Jazzy like that. She's special to me.

Lance: Man, you acting like a punk and not my friend.

After a few more playful words, Cliff told Lance he'd call him back. He went into his bedroom and plugged up his game. As Cliff played his Playstation, thoughts of Jazzy raced through his mind. Jazzy was definitely a beautiful young lady with long black hair and a slender build. He thought about calling his Granny Big, but he did not want to hear the sermon about saving one's self for marriage. The only thing that crossed Cliff's mind was spending a little money to get what he wanted: Sex. Maybe Lance was right.

Cliff's mind began to race. *I've been waiting on this moment for a long time,* thought Cliff. *How could one time hurt anything? Besides, who would know of the act other than me and Jazzy? Surely, she wants me as much as I want her since we have so much fun together.*

The smell of smoke pushed the thoughts of hot

sex out of Cliff's mind for the moment. Cliff opened his dorm door and was bombarded by a fellow colleagues running out of their sleeping quarters. Cliff saw one of his teammates who informed him there was a fire on the third floor due to someone using a hotplate.

After the fire department came and put out the fire and the Fire Marshall gave the clearance, Cliff was happy to be able to return to his dorm. He was tired. He looked at the clock and saw that it was three twenty-eight in the morning, but his mind was on Jazzy.

****

It was spring break on the SCC campus but Jazzy couldn't travel home because she was still required to work in the café. She was not at all disappointed however, because she needed to make some extra cash to buy a car.

Cliff had basketball practice and would be spending most of his time on campus as well. The day after the fire, Cliff stopped by the café to surprise Jazzy on her break.

Cliff: Hey beautiful. Will you accompany me to dinner this evening?
Jazzy: Sure, I will, Cliff. Surely, I will.

Jazzy was excited that the basketball star was not only her guy, but she had a date.... a real date.

Date night finally arrived and Jazzy was anxious to wear her white sundress. On the way out the door, she took a pair of sunglasses from Mary.

Cliff was outside waiting for her in a red Kia Optima with the sun roof open. He looked at the beautiful woman in the white sundress and was mesmerized by her beauty.

Jazzy felt like the luckiest young lady alive. Cliff had planned out the day very well. They had dinner at the Whitfield Steak House and a movie at CBecks Movie Theater.

On the way home, Jazzy noticed that Cliff was taking an unfamiliar route away from the theater. Even though Jazzy grew a little uncomfortable about the change, she did not make a big deal out of it. The next thing she knew, her knight in shining armor had pulled into the parking lot of a Motel Moocha and was walking over to her side of the car.

Jazzy did not know what to do. She liked the way she felt when she was around him. She'd thought of dreams, goals and plans for their future together. All she wanted was Cliff.

She allowed Cliff to guide her into the motel. To her surprise, he had a room key, which meant he'd already reserved the room before their date. Jazzy was scared, but she didn't want to lose the man she'd fallen so deeply in love with. Cliff wasted no time. He began to kiss her almost immediately after they entered the hotel room. Jazzy was afraid. She was a virgin and she hadn't pictured her first time taking place in a Motel Moocha.

The painful and less than pleasant experience was over in a matter of minutes, and Jazzy felt stunned.

Cliff led her out of the hotel room almost immediately after the deed was finished. Jazzy could not say a word. She'd just lost her virginity to a man she loved, but the event was more confusing than loving.

Is this what real love feels like? Jazzy's mind was riddled with questions. Cliff, on the other hand, felt great, even though he did feel bad about removing Jazzy's innocence.

After their sexual encounter, Jazzy began to see less and less of Cliff. A couple of months went by, and Cliff only visited Jazzy every other day, and those visits began to slow down as well. He came up with every reason as to why his routine had changed. Jazzy, on the other hand, began to experience some changes in her body. One day, she was lying on her bed when Mary asked her if she was okay. She'd been sick a lot lately and Mary had taken notice.

Jazzy: I've been having bad headaches and severe stomach cramps. I don't know what's wrong.

Mary: You have been complaining about headaches all week. Do you have migraines?

Jazzy: No, I usually don't have headaches.

There's something wrong with me. I know it is.

Mary: When was the last time you had your monthly cycle?

Jazzy: It has been two months since I've seen my cycle, and I have not had any relations lately. The last time I had a sexual encounter with Cliff was two months ago.

After their talk, Mary volunteered to take Jazzy to the Health Department two miles down the road the following day. Jazzy signed in and was seen by the doctor. Mary and Jazzy sat in the office awaiting the results of a series of tests the doctor had performed on Jazzy. Minutes seemed like hours as the ladies waited in the lobby of the Health Department.

Finally, a voice came from a room nearby. "Ms. Dents?" said the nurse. "We have the results from your pregnancy test."

Broken Promises

Minutes later, a stunned Jazzy walked out of the clinic with the words from the nurse still ringing in her head. *"You are pregnant."*

The ride back to the dorm room was a silent journey. Jazzy's eyes filled with tears, and Mary didn't know what to say to her. Jazzy could only think of Cliff, and what he would say. She could not wait to tell him that they would be having a baby.

Once back in the room, Mary sat on the bed as Jazzy called and told Cliff the news.
"What?" Cliff's voice was loud. "A baby? What are we going to do with a baby?" Cliff's mind began to race. On one hand, he was afraid, but on the other, he was somewhat happy. He knew that he needed to call his mother and that is exactly what he did, and Granny Big reacted just like he knew she would.

Granny Big: Have you both asked the Lord to forgive you because you were not supposed to be having sexual relations before marriage?

Cliff: Yes, we have, Mother. Mother, will you please be happy for us? Please.

Granny Big: You know I am here for y'all in whatever way I'm needed. That does not change the fact that you did this out of order.

It took Granny Big a couple months to grasp the idea that her youngest son was about to have a baby. This was a hard pill to swallow because she had so many dreams for Cliff.

****

A few weeks later, Jazzy had her first sonogram. Neither Cliff nor Jazzy were prepared for what happened next. The doctor began performing the sonogram, and he noticed three small sacks in Jazzy's womb.

Cliff was startled by what he saw on the screen as well.

Cliff: How many babies are we looking at?

Doctor: There seems to be three babies here, Mr. Willis. Based on the positioning of the children, they are definitely identical. You will have your hands full, but you can do it.

Jazzy laid on the bed in disbelief since she had not fully accepted the fact that she was having one baby, but now she was being told she was having three babies. Jazzy's mind immediately went to her mother. She knew that her mother would love to know that she was having grand-babies, but she was living in a nursing home with Alzheimer's disease. Jazzy had not seen her mother for several weeks so she decided to visit her mother the following weekend.

On Saturday morning, Jazzy and Cliff went to Hearts Lane Nursing Plaza to visit her mother,

Glenda. Glenda was sitting outside on the patio talking with a gentleman who appeared to be in his late fifties or early sixties.

Jazzy: Hello, Ms. Fox. Do you know who this person is that is being so patience with my mother? He is really being very kind.
Ms. Fox: Of course, I know who that gentleman is, Jazzy. His name is Isaac Dents.

Jazzy glanced once again through the large patio windows at her mother and the stranger sitting with her. Jazzy's mind raced and her heart began to beat faster and faster. She felt weak and thought she would collapse. The caregiver asked Jazzy if she could get her some water, and Jazzy nodded her head in affirmation. She needed that water and she needed it bad. When the caregiver returned, she brought Jazzy a bottle of water and a wet towel to put on her head.

Jazzy and Cliff introduced themselves to the gentleman and he looked at Jazzy with excitement in his eyes, yet, there was a sadness in his eyes as well. The gentleman stood up and introduced himself

Isaac: I am Isaac Dents. Jazzy, I'm your father.
Jazzy: Um... You are who?

Jazzy began to shake nervously. "I do not have a father," replied Jazzy. "I repeat, I do not have a father." Jazzy wanted to run out of the plaza, but after looking over at her mother, she began to calm down. She had been raised not to be disrespectful to her elders, so Jazzy collected herself and turned to Cliff.

Jazzy: I'm sorry. I apologize.
Cliff: It's okay, baby.
Glenda: This is your father, cupcake. He has visited with me every Saturday since I have been a resident here. I told you when you were

in middle school that I would tell you all that you needed to know once you were old enough to understand. I feel that this is the time.

Jazzy was ashamed, hurt, and curious all at the same time. She was ashamed because she was rude to Isaac initially. She was hurt because for 19 years, she could not remember one birthday card or one visit from her father. Jazzy was curious about the man standing before her. It was obvious that Isaac and Glenda had been communicating because he knew that Glenda was living in the Plaza. Jazzy's mind was full of questions.

Jazzy: Why didn't you ever come and see me?
Isaac: I thought that running was the best thing to do at first. Your mother and I were high school sweethearts. We loved each very much. I can recall the day that my life took a turn for the worse, and I thought that turning to an

alcohol bottle would save me from the pain of it all. I lost my job working as a warden at the Winslow Penitentiary in Florida. The week after I lost my job, my home burned to the ground. The worst part was that I had let the insurance on my home lapse because I spent almost everything I had trying to live a lavish lifestyle. I did not invest in my future because I felt that I had time to turn everything back around.

I believed with everything in me that it would be best if I walked away from everything. I loved Glenda, but I did not want to be a burden to her and my unborn baby girl. I started checking myself into various homeless shelters all over the city of Miami because I was not allowed to stay at a shelter longer than thirty days at a time. Jazzy, that was my lifestyle until two years ago when I saw my childhood friend, Micky, coming out of a McDonald's near the shelter I was living in. I was ashamed when I heard my friend scream my name across the parking lot. My friend said to me, "Hey there. It's been a long time." I greeted him and we started talking about my current situation. That's when Micky said, "I have great news. Don't you have experience working in risk populations?" That was the day my life took a turn for the better. Micky told me about a job working as a case specialist with Youth Court for truancy and gang violence. He took me to his two bedroom apartment and groomed me for the job opportunity.

Once I gained employment, I began to search for my daughter and her mother. I looked for at least a year, and finally, I found Glenda. You had just started college and I was so proud of you. Your mother arranged for me to come over to her place to see some of your pictures and awards. It was during these mini visits that I noticed that something was wrong with Glenda. I could not disappear from her life again when she needed me the most.

I scheduled a doctor's appointment for Glenda and accompanied her to the doctor's office. Her health started to deteriorate rapidly. One day, while cooking Glenda's dinner, I noticed a piece of paper that had a number on it, and that paper had your name on it. I dialed that number often around three o'clock in the morning because I was just settling in around that time, and I hoped you'd be up. The number I dialed was 787-211-2882.

Jazzy: The number you dialed was Granny Big's number. That's my boyfriend's mother.
Isaac: Oh, okay. I was just reaching out. I was trying to find you by any means necessary.

Jazzy could not take any more of the story. To her, it all seemed so unreal. Cliff got Isaac's number and provided him with his number also. Jazzy walked over to her mother and informed her that she was going to be a grandmother, but Glenda did not recognize her at that point.

Jazzy brushed her mother's hair and held her hand. Tears streamed down Jazzy's face as sorrow filled her heart. She needed her mother now more than ever. She did not know the first thing about parenting. She did not know the man who, just moments ago, stated that he was her father. Her mother promised that she would provide her with answers at the right time…. And now was the right time, but her mother's Alzheimer's had shut down her memory yet again. After speaking with her mother and father for another hour, Jazzy and Cliff decided to leave.

****

Jazzy's stomach continued to grow as the months passed. Cliff was growing even more distant day to day, and Jazzy could not understand why. Normally, he would call to inquire about any of her upcoming doctor's appointments or to see if she needed anything, but lately, he'd started missing appointments and would often rush her off the phone anytime she called. Most of the time, he wouldn't answer Jazzy's calls at all. Jazzy was now six months pregnant and the doctor had placed her on bed rest because of the triplets.

Jazzy stayed in touch with Granny Big and kept her informed about her health and the state of the triplets, even when Cliff didn't have a clue.

Cliff was not ready to be a father. He felt like he was not supposed to have children until he had a career and was married. He had recently gained employment at Style N Shoes in the Galleria, and he barely had time for anything else.

One evening when Cliff was at work, he could not help but notice a young lady by the name of Kate. Kate worked at the ice cream shop next door to Cliff's place of employment, and he was instantly attracted to her. The two started having lunch together, and eventually, thoughts of Jazzy faded to black.

Jazzy called Cliff one evening to see if he could help her buy more maternity clothes. She was getting bigger and most of her clothes did not fit her anymore. To her surprise, Cliff began to curse at her. He said that he had just bought clothes for her, and he told her not to call him anymore unless it was related to the children.

Jazzy cried herself to sleep that night. The next day, she called Granny Big to see what she should do. Granny Big prayed with Jazzy and told her she would help her in any way she could.

Broken Promises

Granny Big asked Jazzy for her size and surprised her with a bag of maternity clothes the following day. Granny Big told Jazzy that she had also noticed that Cliff was acting as if he did not have any sense and she did not understand why. She said all she could do was trust that God would bring him back to his first love, and that was the church.

Jazzy kept in touch with her father and the two began to grow close. One day, Mr. Dents asked his daughter if she wanted to meet him for lunch, and she agreed.
Jazzy and her father had just finished lunch when she noticed that her pants were wet. It appeared that she had waste water on her denim shorts.

Isaac: Jazzy, are you experiencing any pain?
Jazzy: No Dad, why do you ask?
Isaac: Are you sure? I got a feeling that you

may be in labor.

Jazzy: I don't think so.

Isaac: Let me take you to get examined anyway. I will feel much better knowing that I am only being paranoid.

The ride to the hospital was a rough one with Isaac speeding in his black Ford Explorer. Luckily, Airlot Hospital was only seven miles away from Olive Sides where they had lunch.

Isaac pulled up on the ramp and emergency staff came out to welcome Jazzy. After her vitals were taken, the doctor decided to keep her for observation. She was later admitted to the hospital due to her blood pressure being really high. Jazzy notified Mary and she, in turn, notified Granny Big. Granny Big came into the hospital room praying that Jazzy's blood pressure would lower. Mary came right after work and stood right by her friend's side, but

Cliff was nowhere to be found.

****

Meagan, Madison and Mallory were born on August 22, but Meagan did not survive because her lungs had not developed properly.

Jazzy blamed herself for Meagan's death. She felt as if she could have eaten and managed her stress levels better. She even wondered why she had looked for love in a man anyway; a man who had left her to deal with the loss of their child alone. Jazzy looked at her two babies and cried so loud that the doctor and nurses cried along with her. Granny Big, Elaine (Jazzy's oldest sister), and Mary were there to support her.

Jazzy was discharged three days after delivering her babies. Isaac picked her up from the hospital and moved her in with him because her apartment would not be ready for another two weeks.

Isaac felt like he owed it to Jazzy to help her get a place to reside in with his grandchildren. Isaac decided in his heart that one thing that he would not miss was the opportunity to be in his grandchildren's lives. Isaac worked, and he needed a little help providing care for his daughter and grandchildren. Mary came over each evening after work to cook and help Jazzy with the babies. Granny Big would help in the mornings.

The first morning that Granny Big came over, she brought bags of items to decorate the girls' nursery. The theme for the room was the Little Princess. Pink and white flowers and tiaras filled the room from wall to wall.

Jazzy was thankful for the downpour of love shown to her by her children's grandmother and her best friend, but she yearned for something else. Although Jazzy had her two babies with her, she felt there was something missing from her life. She didn't understand what it was, but she understood that something was missing.

Chapter 2

The Invisible Wound

Five years would go by, and Cliff still hadn't
been a present force in his children's lives.
The state fair was in town and Granny Big
insisted on taking Madison and Mallory to ride
on the horse carousel, but the morning rain
had her second guessing the trip. The girls
were ready to eat cotton candy. Mallory's
favorite flavor of cotton candy was blueberry.
Granny Big did not inform the girls that their
father was in the car waiting on them.

Cliff had not seen his children because he
moved to Stonyhill, Kansas to work for a meat-
packing plant. Cliff jumped outside of the car
with excitement when he saw his daughters.
The girls were both skipping and holding each

other's hands while going to the car.

All Cliff wanted to do was spend each moment with them until he left on Sunday. He did not have a good relationship with Jazzy. Cliff realized that he had wronged Jazzy all those years ago, but did not know how to say that he was wrong or that he was sorry. He often thought about Jazzy and would often ask around about her. He was now in a relationship, so his thoughts of Jazzy carried no weight. Cliff would ask his mother about his girls, and would send money from time to time to buy the girls a few items.

Jazzy was working as Assistant Manager at a local Target store. She still lived with her father on the outskirts of town at his farm with chickens, cows and a few hogs. Jazzy loved living on the farm. It was her newfound safe haven. The sound of the birds in the morning and the peaceful sunset was all she needed to keep a sound mind. Not to mention, the neighbors were just like family to her. The Lonsees were the reason she did not have to pay for a babysitter.

Mrs. Janey Lonsee provided care for Madison and Mallory to allow Jazzy to save money. From the time Janey saw Jazzy, she was drawn to her smile and outgoing spirit. Jazzy viewed Mrs. Janey as a grandmother for her children since her mother was unable to enjoy life due to health limitations. For some strange reason, she felt warmth in her heart when around Mrs. Janey.

Isaac enjoyed having his daughter and grandchildren with him because it made him feel youthful and fulfilled. Jazzy told him that she would be moving out the following June once she'd saved enough money to rent one of her boss's rental properties.

Jazzy thought it was a good idea since the home was only three miles from her job and five miles from the Head-start the twins would be attending. The area was nothing like the projects that Jazzy was raised in, plus she would no longer have to rely on laundry mats. The home would have washer and dryer hook-ups. Jazzy was at a point in her life where she felt like she was at an all-time high because she was becoming independent.

One day, while Jazzy was at work, she noticed a policeman was headed in her direction. Jazzy thought to herself, *what has one of my co-workers done now?*

Officer: Are you Jazzy Dents?

Jazzy: Yes, I am.

Officer: We need you to ride with us to the hospital, please.

Jazzy: Why do I need you to take me to the hospital?

The Invisible Wound

Officer: Ma'am, please. Please come with me. Are you related to Isaac Dents?

Jazzy: Yes, Isaac is my father.

Officer: There has been an accident and your father was involved.

Jazzy grabbed her purse and hurried out the door.

****

At the hospital, Jazzy was asked to speak with the chaplain and then asked to identify her father. Jazzy felt as if her heart was going to jump out of her chest. Her legs began to feel like jello, and she fainted. Isaac Dents had died instantly from a hit and run in the parking lot of B & B Wholesale.

Mary was right by her friend's side and could not imagine going through all that her friend had endured in the short time that she had known her.

Jazzy: Mary, how is it that everyone has brought me cards to make me feel better when all that is mentioned is this God? Tell me.

Mary: God is right there with you, Jazzy. He is always there.

Jazzy: If He is so good, then why am I loosing everyone who means the world to me? My dad was not perfect, but he tried to get it right. He had plans for Madison and Mallory. He had plans… He had plans.

At that moment, Mary hugged her friend and held her while the two of them sobbed together. Jazzy was stronger than she thought she was. She did not understand the emptiness that she felt, but she knew it could not last forever. Mary spent the night at Jazzy's house to help with getting the children fed and into bed.

Jazzy: I don't understand. I don't understand why this is happening to me. I try to live right, but it seems like my world is falling to the ground.

Mary: Jazzy, you have to pray because God does not make mistakes. He really don't, Jazzy. Will you come to church with me this Sunday? I don't have all the answers, but maybe my pastor can answer some of the questions that you may have.

Jazzy: I'm not ready to do the church thing. I'm not knocking how you are doing things at all but....

Mary: But what, Jazzy? Will you come with me? Or at least think about it.

****

Sunday finally came, and Mary was watching the United Wings Ministries show while getting ready for church when she heard her phone ring. Mary was not expecting anyone to be calling at this hour.

Mary: Hello.

Jazzy: Hey, chile; what's up with you?

Mary: Just getting ready for church. What are you doing?

Jazzy: I was wondering if you could pick us up for church this morning?

Mary: Yes, will you be ready in fifteen minutes? I don't like to be late, okay?

Jazzy: Do you think I would have you late? Besides I asked you to pick me up.

Jazzy enjoyed herself at church. The church had a great youth ministry and there were no words for the sermon that was preached on that day. It almost seemed as though the pastor was talking directly to Jazzy. The sermon was entitled, *Blind, But Now I See*. The choir sang songs of Zion, and Jazzy had to step outside of church because she felt very emotional. It was something about that message that pricked Jazzy's heart. Whatever it was, she made up in her mind that she would definitely be returning… real soon.

Chapter 3

Picked Lock

Jazzy was excited about finally being moved into her three bedroom home on Lorain's Avenue in spite of all the rain in the forecast. Mallory was in the kitchen learning how to cook meatball spaghetti when there was a knock on the door. Jazzy went to the door to see who was there.

It was a delivery guy from UPS bringing a package addressed to Mallory and Madison. Jazzy saw that the packages were from Granny Big, so she handed the boxes to the twins and turned back to the UPS guy. The children turned around to open their boxes while Jazzy signed for the packages.

The UPS guy expressed that he thought Jazzy was very attractive and asked if he could exchange numbers with her. As he was speaking, he began writing his number on a piece of cardboard, and then he handed the makeshift business card to her. The name written on the cardboard was Milton Turniseet. Jazzy told him that she would be in touch.

Jazzy decided to give Milton a call on the drive home from work the next day. Milton answered on the second ring.

Milton: Hello? Hello?

Jazzy: Hey… hey! This is Jazzy. How are you?

Milton: Oh, so Ms. playing hard to get is not really so hard to get? *(Laughs)*. I'm glad to hear your voice, and a nice one it is.

Jazzy: I was just making sure that you gave me the right number. I've been burned a time or two with that game. So…

Milton: So, what are your plans for the evening? Booster Barbecue Shack is having a grand opening this evening at six. Are you interested in going? Or maybe we can go to a park and just talk.

Jazzy: I promised my daughters that I would take them to the park, and I cannot let them down. We usually go to the park once a week to feed the ducks, and the girls just love the swings. In fact, I love to swing.

Milton: I don't mind joining you all for an evening at the park. I can stop and grab some snow cones at the little hut right down the street. Should I pick up anything for you?

Jazzy: No, I'm good. I'll call you after I pick my children up from the sitter.

Milton: Okay, just say the word and I'll be there in dash.

Jazzy sat in silence as she hung up the phone. She could not believe she was allowing herself to let someone call her. Furthermore, she was letting a guy be around her precious jewels... her children. Jazzy played this decision over

and over again in her mind and finally decided
that it was okay. She told herself that it was just
the park and a friendly conversation while the
children played.

****

Mallory and Madison realized they were pulling
into the park, and the girls began to scream for
joy. They began to bounce around and smile
from ear to ear. Jazzy gave them both the go
ahead to get out of the car, and their first stop
was the swings.

Moments later, Jazzy heard a loud whistle
across the park. When she looked up, she saw
Milton with a bouquet of tulips in his hand and
a picnic basket in the other. Jazzy didn't know
if she should walk towards him or sit still. She
feared she would fall on her face if she moved.

She smiled while Milton sat the goodies down

by the park's bench. Milton then told Jazzy that he would be right back. When he returned, he had a pepperoni pizza and two watermelon snow cones.

Jazzy: How did you know the girls' favorite flavor of snow cone? I did not mention that to you.

Milton: Awe, lady bug... I know everything.

Jazzy: *(Chuckles)* Yea right. Mallory and Madison come on so you can eat, babies. Mallory.....Madison. Come on.

Mallory and Madison enjoyed having Milton around.

****

Months later, Milton moved in with Jazzy and the girls, and became a beneficial part of the family's life. Milton paid the majority of the bills and provided care for the children as Jazzy worked. Jazzy had just started a new job working 12 hour shifts, and this was a big change for the girls. Ms. Lonsee was still a grandmother figure to the girls, but now she was up in age. Arthritis, hearing loss, and the loss of eyesight were all setting in. Milton would go to see Mrs. Lonsee if he had any trouble with the girls, and he would often get recipes from her to prepare the meals.

Things began to grow sour between Milton and Jazzy. One night, when Jazzy was asleep, Milton walked into the room with the girls and adjusted their covers on the bed. This behavior seemed normal at first, but Jazzy had taught her daughters that if something in their being (gut) did not feel right, then it's not right. Madison began to feel uneasy, but she pretended to be asleep.
Milton came back into the room, but this time, he slid the pink and white comforter back

slowly and rubbed his hands across Madison's private area. Madison felt violated and turned over in the bed to see Milton fleeing the room. Madison did not know what to do.

Was she dreaming? She began to think about how the way her uncles hugged her didn't feel wrong. She often received hugs from other adults who didn't make her feel this way. So, what was different? Madison knew what she needed to do. Madison's heart raced as she got closer to her mother's door. The closer she got to her mother's room, the louder her mother's snoring sounded. Ordinarily, her mother didn't snore, but she was tired from working all those long hours at work. Nevertheless, Madison knew her mother was never too tired for her.

Madison: Momma, Momma. Can I tell you something?

Jazzy: Hey, baby. Of course you can. What's wrong? Jump in my bed and talk to me. What's wrong, Maddie.

Madison: You said that I can tell you anything, right?

Jazzy: Yes, what's wrong?

(Jazzy sits up in her bed.)

Madison: I was lying in my bed, and I felt somebody rub their fingers across my underwear, Momma. Um... then I turned over and saw Milton leaving my room really fast.

Jazzy: He did what? And where the heck is he right now? Know that you have not done anything wrong, baby. I'm so sorry.

Madison: *(Cries)* Momma I'm so scared.

Jazzy and Madison walked down the hall into the living room where Milton pretended to be asleep. Jazzy grabbed him by the neck and demanded that he get out. Madison ran into the kitchen to call the police. Milton tried to flee from Jazzy, but tripped because his shoes were untied and hit his head. He was unconscious until the police arrived.

By the time the police arrived, Milton was conscious, but still dazed. He was immediately arrested and taken to jail. As it turned out, Milton had previous charges of child molestation in the states of Alabama and Kansas. Officer Joey stated that Milton had been on the run from the law for a long time.

Jazzy was enraged, especially at herself. How could she trust someone around her children and not know what he was truly about? How could she leave a man with her most prized possessions, and how would she ever earn the trust of Madison again?

Jazzy cried and cried. While she cried, thoughts of her childhood came into her mind.

She realized that the same thing had happened to her when she was a child, but she had not confided in anyone. At that time, she'd felt that she did not want to hurt the perpetrator, who was a family friend. Jazzy wondered if she would have had a better childhood if she had confided in her mother. She had dealt with that summer day as if it had never happened. She'd escaped that monster, only to have that monster try to hunt her daughter as its next prey.

Jazzy hugged Madison and they cried together as Jazzy repeatedly apologized.

Madison said, "Cliff was supposed to protect me from bad people, but he was a bad person."

Jazzy could not stop apologizing to her daughter, but Madison looked at her mother and told her that she was the best mother in the world. Jazzy screamed and laughed at the same time.

"I hope that I can one day live up to that title," she said. "I wish."

Chapter 4

The Drift

Kyle Sharpe, an engineer from Boston, Massachusetts, came to his hometown to help build a bypass. Kyle had not visited his hometown in ten years. The last time he'd came to Boston, he'd come to visit his daddy on the family farm. Kyle drove up to his father's farm, and to his surprise, he saw a young lady who resembled his father, but he did not recognize her. He walked up to the door and asked for Isaac. Jazzy informed him that Isaac had passed away three years ago. Kyle fell down to his knees after falling over a plant that Jazzy had potted.

After Kyle regained his composure, he wanted to know who Jazzy was and what happened to his father. Jazzy invited him into the house and asked him to follow her to the living room to sit down. She then brought him a glass of water.

Jazzy: Hello, I am Jazzy Dents. Isaac was my father.

Kyle: What do you mean that Isaac was your father? Isaac is my father.

Jazzy : That would make you my brother, and what's your name?

Kyle: I am Kyle Dents Sharpe. What happened to my father? Where is my dad?

Jazzy: Kyle, dad passed away three years ago in a hit and run accident. He died instantly. He did not suffer at all.

Kyle: I did not know. How could I be so stupid? I did not take the time to visit the old man like I should have. The last time I spoke with him was nine years ago. I love that guy. I will miss him tremendously.

Jazzy: I will too. So where are you from?

Kyle: I am residing in Boston right now, but I

am seriously considering moving back home. I have been all over the world but ain't nothing like home.

Kyle spent the rest of the morning getting to know his sister and nieces. Later that afternoon, Jazzy took her daughters to visit with their grandmother. Ms. Glenda did not recognize them, but the girls brushed their grandmother's hair and sang songs with her as they played from her black am/fm radio.

It was funny how she knew the words to the gospel song *I Can't Give Up Now* by Lee Williams, but could not remember her own name. It was almost as if power from on high had joined in with her while she sung.

Jazzy spoke with the caregiver and was informed that her mother Alzheimer's was getting worse. Jazzy thanked the caregiver for updating her with her mother's health condition, and she left the nursing home with a heavy heart.

Later that day, Jazzy finished gathering the remainder of her father's belongings and placed them in the garage to donate to Will & Things the next day. As she walked from her car, she saw headlights pulling in behind her car. It was her brother, Kyle.

Kyle had just finished meeting with community leaders to map out zoning for the new bypass. He had initially planned to spend his time in town with his father, so he hadn't booked a room at any hotel

Kyle: Hey there. I was wondering, would it be okay if I bunked here for the evening? I know I should have mentioned it to you earlier, but you caught me off guard with all of the news you'd told me earlier. I'll pay room and board if I must.

Jazzy: Now, you are my brother. What do I look like charging you to lay your head down at our father's house? You are as welcomed in our father's home as I am. The girls and I are excited to know that we have more family. How long will you be visiting?

Kyle: Maybe a month. I may be moving back to town; I'm not sure yet. I have been all over the world, and I'm a little tired of the fast life.

Jazzy: Oh, okay. I see.

****

Kyle could not stop coughing. Water did not ease the rapid, dry cough and cough drops didn't work either. Kyle knew that it could only mean that his health was getting worse. At work one day, Kyle had passed out and blamed it on exhaustion. When rushed to the hospital by ambulance, it was revealed that his oxygen levels were only 87 percent. He was admitted and later released after several breathing treatments and medication. For several weeks, he'd noticed that he would have a cough here and there, but would regain his breathing rhythm quickly. But today, was a different story.

Jazzy: Kyle, dinner's ready. Kyle?

Madison: Uncle Ky, Momma said that we can eat. She's through with dinner.

Kyle: Okay sweetheart, tell your mother to put my plate up for later because I'm a little tired. Okay?

Madison: Okay, Uncle. I'll tell her.

Later that day, Jazzy was running late for work, and when she walked outside, she noticed that Kyle was already gone. Jazzy needed someone to give her car a boost. Mr. Lonsee was home, so she walked down to the neighbor's house to see if he could help her out. Mr. Lonsee got the car started and told Jazzy to not cut the car off until she got to work. He further told her to call him approximately an hour before she got off for the evening so he could make sure her car was okay for travel. Jazzy agreed.

An hour before she got off work, Jazzy called Mr. Lonsee.

Jazzy: Hey. Mr. Lonsee, this is Jazzy. I was calling to let you know that my brother, Kyle, took my car to have a new battery put in it.
Mr. Lonsee: I'm glad he did. Do you have a ride to get home from work then?
Jazzy: Yes, he left his car with me so I can just drive home while he's getting mine worked on.
Mr. Lonsee: Well, I just wanted to make sure because you do have those babies to take places, and you need your car to be able to get around. You know we love you and those

babies.

Jazzy: I know, Mr. Lonsee. Thank you for everything.

Kyle picked Madison and Mallory up from school, and by that time, it was time to pick Jazzy up from work. For dinner, Kyle treated his new found family to Papa Jamie on 78th Street. It had been a thriving and popular joint when Kyle resided there, but now, it was the hang out spot for teens.

Madison and Mallory loved pizza, so that's what they got. Jazzy ordered lemon pepper chicken wings and Kyle said that he was not hungry. They used this time together to talk about their day and the years prior to them meeting. Kyle had two children, a boy and a girl. Both children lived in Boston with their mother. Kyle was very active in their lives, but he was always traveling the country with his job.

****

Jazzy woke up to Mallory hollering for her to get up. Mallory was screaming that Uncle Kyle was on the bathroom floor coughing and balled up in a knot. When Jazzy found him, he was almost out of breath. Finally, Kyle was able to point in the direction of his room, asking for Madison to bring Jazzy his breathing pump. Jazzy hooked up the machine and Kyle started to breathe better but he was very weak.

Kyle told Jazzy about the issues surrounding his health. Kyle informed Jazzy that he had grown concerned about the coughing spells and the frequency of them. Kyle then said he would like to schedule an appointment with a doctor to have some testing done to see what exactly was going on. Jazzy called Dr. Todd to schedule an appointment for her brother. The receptionist scheduled an appointment for Kyle at nine thirty on Thursday morning.

****

Kyle: I am a little nervous, Jazzy. I know I am supposed to pray, and I have. My mother told me as a young boy to trust Him even when I can't trace Him. I just don't know, Jazzy. What if the doctor tells me some very bad news?

Jazzy: What if they don't say anything is wrong? We will not worry about anything before they inform us. Okay?

Kyle: They will tell us something, Jazzy. I have known for a year now that I have a spot on my lungs, and after Dr. Knocks told me the news… I just did not go back to the doctor. Instead, I walked around trying to act like I didn't know. I was in denial, sis. It did not become real to me until I fell over in your bathroom, Jazzy. That's when I knew it was real.

Jazzy: A spot? A spot of what? What are you

telling me?

Kyle: Jazzy, I have a spot on my lung. Prior to that diagnosis, I was told by another doctor that I have a small tumor in my chest cavity. I did not wait around to see what the spot was because I feared the worst. I was only 37 at the time, and I felt I had my entire life ahead of me. I'm sorry. I am sorry for coming here with my problems, but I was looking for my dad. Instead, I was blessed to have a chance to see my sister and nieces. I have walked around in denial, and for some strange reason, I thought that I could outrun the problem. Well, it's obvious that I can't run any longer because I have started to have symptoms that I did not have before.

Jazzy: Let's just see what the doctor says on Thursday. In the meantime, take a warm shower and try to relax.

The room was very dim and quiet. The

receptionist welcomed Kyle and presented him with documents to complete for first time visitors. Jazzy assisted him with the paperwork because he was tired. By then, Kyle was having to take breathing treatments three times a day.

"Mr. Sharpe, the doctor will see you now," said Nurse Polly. Jazzy accompanied Kyle to the examination room.

The drive home was very silent. Kyle's eyes were fixed outside the window and Jazzy was driving, but another force controlled the steering of the wheel.

Mallory and Madison were sitting under the big oak tree feeding the swans near the pond when Kyle and Jazzy made it home from the doctor's appointment. Kyle hugged the girls and started feeding the swans with them. Jazzy went into the house to prepare a quick dinner: Sloppy Joe's with a side of French fries.

Kyle: Nieces, I have something serious that I need to tell you. I want you guys to know that I love you and I am so glad that we were able to meet. I also want to let you know that the doctor says that I am a very sick man. *(Kyle begins coughing)*. The doctor's visit today revealed that cancer is now in my chest cavity and in one of my lungs. They said that I may have six months to a year to live. *(Kyle voice begins to shake as he cried)*.

Mallory: Don't cry, Uncle. Don't cry. You sure the doctor knows what he's talking about?

Kyle: Yes, they are very sure, baby. I'm scared. I had plans to get married again and have more children. I want to be around to see you all get grown and have a family. I know I need to pray. But it's so hard.

Mallory: Uncle, if you know you need to pray, then I believe that's what you should do.

Kyle: Ain't no use, Mal. Why did I have to end up with cancer? I have a lot of things to do. I just don't understand.

****

It was a cool fall day in Coverdale when Kyle decided to visit his childhood friend, Reagan. Reagan had not moved from the small community after high school. He worked at the local court house and was now running for Mayor. Kyle was so proud of his friend. Reagan was the kind of guy that, if you needed him, he was there. Kyle pulled up under the shade tree near the picnic table where Reagan and his youngest son, Jolby, sat. Reagan jumped up and ran towards his friend with a big smile on his face. Reagan had not seen Kyle since graduation.

Reagan: Man, look what the wind blew in. It's going to storm today. I haven't seen you in twenty years.

Kyle: I know, bro. I'm in town for a while, and I

needed to see you. I was sitting back at dad's house, and I got to reminiscing about the good old days. Remember when I almost got expelled from school for taking the keys to the science lab from Mr. Brits?

Reagan: Yes, indeed. I was so scared that your daddy was going to beat my behind and yours, even though I had nothing to do with it. But because your dad knew we were always together, he said I played a role in the malice.

Kyle: So, that's your little man there?

Reagan: Yes, that's my one and only son and my only child. I've always wanted more than one, but the wife don't want any more children until this election is over.

Kyle: Well, I have two children: a boy and girl. I'm divorced now and considering moving back here. I have a lot going on, and I just don't know.

Reagan: So, do you want to go for a ride? Do you need to talk? Let me take Junior in the house to his mother, and we will hop in the old pick up and ride like old times.

****

Reagan sat on the tailgate of his truck as Kyle told him of his father's passing and how he'd ended back up in town. Kyle further informed his friend about the life-threatening disease he was battling. Reagan continued to listen as his friend poured out the issues of his heart. Even though he was very quiet, Reagan was deeply saddened by the news of his friend having cancer. Furthermore, the hurt he saw in Kyle's eyes as he spoke of his illness was tearing at his heart. Kyle stated that he was scared, and at that point, Reagan knew that he needed to give him a word from the Lord.

Reagan: Kyle? I would like you to go somewhere with me on Wednesday night if you don't have plans.

Kyle: I don't really have plans. I just get up and do what I feel like doing *(coughs)*. Where are you trying to take me, bro?

Reagan: I was wondering if you would go to bible study with me. I enjoy bible study, and don't worry, you can wear casual clothing if you want to. You know, we have that, "come as you are" rule there.

Kyle: You mean, I don't have to wear a suit? Cause if I did, I would have to turn you down.

Reagan: I feel like you need to hear the Word. For some reason, when I feel down or I'm going through an ordeal, those words tend to make it all better. It's worth a try.

Kyle: Yes, it is worth a try.

****

Kyle invited Jazzy and the girls to attend bible study with him and his friend, Reagan. Jazzy had never really attended church as an adult and was not all that excited about going. But to keep her brother happy, she agreed to go. Church was located on the country side of town, and about 30 people were in attendance. The smiles and hugs won Madison and Mallory over. Madison adored receiving hugs, and she loved giving them. Two of the girls in Mallory and Madison's class were at church and called for them as they entered the sanctuary. Jazzy allowed the teens to sit with their friends, and she went to sit on the pews with Kyle and Reagan.

As the Word went forth, Kyle was encouraged. "Whatever this feeling is, it feels good," he said.

After church, Jazzy hurried home to warm up leftovers from the night before. Sweet potatoes, pork roast, and rice were on the menu, and corn bread was in the oven. Jazzy told the girls that dinner would be ready in ten minutes. Madison told Mallory that it was time to eat and proceeded to called for Kyle, but he did not answer. Madison walked to Kyle's room and noticed that he had collapsed at the foot of his bed. Madison hurried to be by Kyle's side and she ended up tripping over the rug near where he laid and bumped her head. Kyle's room was a mess; his clothes were scattered everywhere. She had never noticed that his room was in such disarray. When she regained her balance, she screamed for her mother to call an ambulance.

Jazzy: Kyle, answer me. Kyle? Kyle? What happened? Open your eyes for me. Please squeeze my hand. Please. Lord, please help me. Don't let my brother die. Please.
Madison: Uncle Ky, please wake up.

Kyle tried to open his eyes. He attempted to squeeze Jazzy's hand, but was too weak. Jazzy held her brother's hand until the ambulance pulled into the garage. Mallory and Jazzy rode to the hospital with him.

After a series of tests were performed, it was confirmed that Kyle was very ill and that the cancer had started to spread. Dr. Todd informed Jazzy that Kyle's cancer had gotten worse. He now had cancer of the lungs, chest cavity and a spot on his brain. Jazzy tried to hold her composure but the news was unbearable.

****

Walking to Kyle's room was tough. The white lab jackets that the doctors wore and the beeping noises from the machines echoed throughout the hospital. Kyle's room was in ICU, right in front of the nurses' station. Per doctor's orders, anyone who came to visit Kyle would have to wear a mask, jacket and gloves. He was placed on isolation for 24 hours.

The Drift

Mallory and Madison drove to the hospital to see their uncle.

Madison's eyes were swollen from crying and Mallory had a faraway stare. Once they arrived at the hospital, they got their passes and went into Kyle's room. Madison came into the room and held her uncle's hand. She began to sing *How Great is Our God* to him. Kyle loved this song. He had this song on repeat in his vehicle.

Jazzy started waving her hands in the air because she saw her brother attempting to open his eyes. The sounds of her shouting could be heard outside the room.

"Glory! Glory to God. My brother is going to be just fine. Thank you, Jesus," she shouted. Tears streamed down Madison and Mallory's face as they witnessed Kyle open his eyes. He tried to speak, but his voice was very raspy and low.

Kyle: What happened to me? Where am I?

Madison: Uncle, you are in the hospital. You passed out in your room, but you are going to be okay.

Kyle: I am ready to go home, Madison. Can you hand me my clothes so I can get dressed?

Jazzy: Kyle, you are not going home today because they want to conduct more tests, okay? You will be allowed to go home after testing. I promise.

****

It was now two weeks since Kyle had been admitted to the hospital. Rain was in the forecast, and the city was experiencing high winds. Tornadoes had been spotted in the surrounding counties. Kyle had been in the hospital for two weeks by then, and was scheduled to be discharged that day.

He had lost over fifteen pounds and was a bit frail. His facial hair was not groomed and his

nails were brittle. Kyle looked in the mirror at
himself and became sad.

Mallory and Madison picked Kyle up from the
hospital because Jazzy had to open up the
store that morning. Madison helped the nurse
put Kyle in the car while Mallory placed his
clothes and get well gifts in the car.

At home, Kyle wanted something to eat so the
girls treated him to a grilled chicken salad and
a bottle of water. Jazzy went to talk with Kyle,
who was sitting on the patio. Kyle was looking
sad and Jazzy wanted to know why.

Jazzy: Why are you staring off in space,
brother?
Kyle: Well, Jazzy, I am a sick man. I am tired
of feeling the way that I feel. Chemotherapy is
taking a toll on me and I'm so tired. I look
around at you all, and I am so thankful that
God allowed our paths to cross. You are a

phenomenal sister and my nieces… words cannot express how much I love them. They have been right by my side, and I am thankful.

Jazzy: Kyle, don't talk like that. I need you to be around for me. I need you.

Kyle: You will be just fine. The doctors told me that I have a very progressive form of cancer. The doctors have given me six months to live and the chemo is not working. So, what am I to do?

Jazzy: You are always talking about praying and going to church, so let's go to church this Sunday.

Kyle: Okay. I will.

****

Sunday finally came and the twins helped load Kyle into the car while Jazzy was locking up the house. While at church, Jazzy saw a group of older women dressed in all white. Her attention was drawn to one particular lady.

She stared at the woman for a long time, and it dawned on her that she did not know the woman at all. The lady looked much like her mother, Glenda. Oh, how she missed her mother. The sound of the piano and drums got Jazzy's attention. The smell of spice and moth balls filled the atmosphere. The choir came into the choir stand with blue and white robes on, and they began singing songs of Zion. One of the songs was one that Jazzy had heard many times in her youth, and now, Mallory and Madison were rocking with the tune. Kyle was sitting next to Madison, holding on to his bible and watching the singers.

The pastor taught a message entitled *Eternity is Near.* Kyle was very attentive to the message, but there was one thing that stood out in his mind. The pastor closed the text with a question. *If you died this moment, where would you spend eternity?*

What was it about this question that bothered Kyle? Kyle was no stranger to the church. In fact, his mother was a devoted Sunday school teacher.

On the drive home, Kyle wanted to get a cream cheese cake. Jazzy pulled into the parking lot of LaLa's Pastries. Mallory and Madison purchased cupcakes, but Jazzy was dieting.

Jazzy had prepared dinner before going to church. She'd cooked baked chicken, rolls, white rice, and green peas. They swallowed the meal down with grape Kool-Aid.
While eating dinner, Kyle could hear that question he'd heard the pastor asking ringing in his head. He thought to himself, *the truth is: if I died at this moment, I would burst hell wide open*.
Kyle had never accepted Jesus as his Lord and Savior. He'd gotten baptized because he'd

felt that it was expected of him by his parents. He did not understand it all, but he knew he needed something or someone to make his life complete. He needed something.

Chapter 5

The Choice

It was going to be a month to remember. Prom dues, dresses, later curfews, and the finals were now the main focus of Madison and Mallory. The girls were happy to be chosen as President and Vice President of their class. The prom theme would be *A Night to Remember.*

Jazzy was busy picking up shoes, panty hose, nail polish, and other glamor items for her girls. She'd taken a day off from work to make sure the young ladies had everything needed to make the upcoming events a joyous, yet memorable time.

Back at the house, Kyle was sitting in the lounger watching television when he started feeling light-headed and fell out of the chair. It was almost three o'clock in the afternoon when the mail carrier discovered Kyle unconscious in the living room.

Mr. Terry (the mail carrier) had heard a dog barking continuously. It was the constant barking of an otherwise quiet dog that prompted him to look inside the storm door, and that's when he saw Kyle's legs stretched out on the floor. He ran back to his delivery van and called for an ambulance.

Madison and her friend Jersey arrived at the house while the ambulance was loading Kyle to take him to the hospital. Madison got out of her friend's black mustang and pushed her way into the ambulance. Uncle Kyle couldn't be sick again. Earlier that morning when Madison had seen her Uncle, he was fine. Additionally, he'd promised to be Madison's escort for prom night, and Uncle Kyle never broke promises.

The Choice

Madison: Uncle Kyle, I'm here with you. Hang in there. We need you around. You are going to be just fine.

Kyle: I am going fishing. They are going to take me to the store to buy a ring, and I'll fly tomorrow.

Madison: Uncle, what are you talking about? It's not making sense.

The paramedic then explained to Madison that her uncle's thoughts were all jumbled. Madison stood next to her uncle and cried. Jersey followed the ambulance to the hospital while Madison contacted her mother and her sister. They were just a few blocks away, and they pulled up while the ambulance was still in front of their home.

****

Kyle said that he felt fine, but tests revealed that his cancer had spread all over his brain and that his health was quickly deteriorating. The doctor's informed Jazzy that Kyle would be assigned hospice care, and that they should make him very comfortable. Jazzy knew that Kyle's health was critical, but she did not know how severe it was.

Kyle spent several days at the hospital before being released to go home. A chaplain was assigned to speak with him. The entire time the chaplain spoke with Kyle, all Kyle could think about was the question the pastor had asked: *If you died this day, where would you spend eternity?*

Mallory and Madison left the hospital to go home and prepare for their special night. Mallory wore a silver dress and clear heels, and her makeup was flawless. Mallory walked down the hall to Madison's room to check on her and saw her sister lying across the bed.

The Choice

Mallory: Hey, are you not going to the prom?

Madison: No, I'm going to stay home. I have too much on my mind. I'm worried about Uncle Kyle.

Mallory: I know that you are, but what about your special night, Maddie? I know you want Uncle to get better. He is in the hospital; they will provide care for him there.

Madison: Yeah, I know. He was supposed to escort me on tonight. He promised that nothing would stand in the way. I'm so tired of every father figure that's supposed to be around always leaving. I'm so tired. I don't want him sick.

Mallory: I understand, but his sickness is beyond our control. All that we can do is pray and put him on the prayer list at church so other believers can pray for him.

Madison: I pray for him. I pray for him all the time. I just don't feel like going, Mal. Have a great time. Take plenty of pictures. I'm going to sleep.

Back at the hospital, Kyle was wide awake in his bed watching *Sanford and Son*. He laughed and slept a while. He was sedated to ease his pain. Kyle murmured to Jazzy that he was ready to give his heart to the Lord.

Jazzy screamed with excitement. She had been praying that God would truly save her brother's soul. Jazzy cried tears of joy because Kyle had finally confessed that he believed in God. He was in his right mind long enough to know that he needed a Savior. She called for the chaplain and Kyle was baptized in the tub at the hospital. He had finally made the choice to choose life over spiritual death.

Kyle was later released from the hospital, and three weeks later, he became very ill and never recovered. He died in his room with the hospice nurse, the chaplain, Jazzy, Madison, and Mallory by his bedside.

Chapter 6

The Shedding of Layers

After the death of Kyle, Madison grieved inwardly. Kyle was not the first male who'd left her feeling empty. Her father had walked out of her life early; her grandfather had reappeared, only to die unexpectedly, her step-father had betrayed her, and now, cancer had claimed the life of her beloved uncle. Madison walked around for a long period of time masking the real pain she was tormented by daily. It appeared that she was coping with everything.

One day, while going through the motions of attending class at community college, Madison saw a handsome, well-dressed, and well-groomed gentleman who caught her eye. He looked familiar, but she was not sure how she knew him. She suddenly realized that he had been in one of her classes last semester. The young man caught Madison staring at him, so he approached her.

"My name is Jette, and who are you?"

Madison: Hi. I'm Madison.

Jette: I saw you watching me from across the way. Are you a student here?

Madison: Yes, I am. My sister and I started last fall. We have enjoyed our time here so far. How long have you been here?

Jette: I no longer attend school here, but I'm visiting my cousin this week to partake in the spring festivities here on campus.

Madison: Oh, I see. You are here to have some fun.

Jette: Yes, I believe in having fun, and to be honest, there isn't anything in life more important to me than having fun, so fun it is.

Madison: Well, I am headed to class. Maybe I'll see you around campus this evening.

The Shedding of Layers

Jette: Yes, I'll be looking forward to talking to you soon.

****

The heat from the sun had Madison so hot that she sweated while walking across the campus from her Business class. The wind was not blowing at all. She could hear the sound of the band playing, and cars were lined up on the sides of the street as far as her eyes could see. She could not wait until her sister left work, so they could meet up with their best friends to enjoy the remainder of the evening.

Madison saw someone waving in her direction from the snow cone vendor stand. She acted as if she did not see the figure in the distance. The more she tried to ignore it, the louder the voice grew. Just as she was about to yell back, her sister ran up to beside her.
Mallory was so beautiful. She had pretty black

curls and pink lip gloss on to accent her full lips. She had on an all white scrub because she had just gotten off work from her new job at the Children's Clinic.

Madison loved her sister so much. Just as the girls were about to head for the café, Jette jogged up beside the girls. Mallory did not know him so she started walking faster. Madison laughed because her sister was not taking any chances.

Madison: Mallory, this is Jette. Jette,this is my sister, Mallory.

Mallory: Oh, okay. So, how do you two know each other?

Jette: We met today, and I would like to hang out with your sister, if that is okay with you.

Mallory: Well, that's all up to Madison because she knows if she wants to spend her time with you or not. I wouldn't know that.

The Shedding of Layers

Madison: I really don't know you, but I don't
see anything wrong with hanging out with you
during the festival. Besides, Mallory can join
us.

The smell of funnel cakes filled the air as
Mallory, Madison, and Jette walked to the inner
court of the campus to listen to the jazz band
play. Jette stopped at the vendor's stand and
purchased a turkey's leg and a funnel cake,
while Madison and Mallory looked for seating
under the huge, red tent.
The band sounded really good. Jette joined the
girls and immediately started dancing. He was
a great dancer. When Madison saw that he
could groove on the dance floor, she was all
smiles.

After hanging out on the campus, Jette
surprised Madison with a romantic picnic at a
park nearby. He had strawberries, grapes,

cheese, crackers, and a bottle of wine. Madison was no drinker, so Jette told her that ladies sip. The wine was so tasteful that she almost drank it all in one setting. They talked with each other, and after a short time, it seemed as if they had known each other forever. The birds were singing and the crickets were chirping, and the sounds set the mood of the night.

For a moment, being in Jette's company erased past hurts and disappointments. It wasn't long before Madison was telling Jette her life's story. Eventually, he became a very good friend to Madison. Whenever he was in town, he would stop in to see her and make sure things were going good in her world.

One Christmas Eve night, Jette brought Madison a gift. He had been drinking so Madison would not let him leave. The night started off with the friends watching movies together while eating dinner, but the night yielded much more. Being young and vulnerable, Madison lost her virginity to her friend.

Madison loved Jette, but she felt violated because Jette did not view her as a girlfriend. She had always envisioned him as more than a friend. Over time, she began to grow resentful because she felt humiliated and disappointed with herself. Madison knew that she needed something to fill the void she was feeling. She didn't know how to fill that void, but she knew that she needed something.

Chapter 7

Unforgettable

Madison enjoyed working for one of the best clothing stores in her community. Tourists from all ages and ethnic groups trusted her and viewed her as an expert in the clothing arena. She had just been promoted to manager for helping the company meet their sale's goals and for being punctual. The truth of the matter was: Madison was a workaholic.

All too often, her friends would tell her that she needed to live a little, and they would try to set her up on blind dates, but she would not comply. The only thing on her mind was providing for her three year old daughter, Alexis.

Alexis's father was very supportive of her.

Madison and David were proud to be parents, but they could not make their relationship work. But the one thing they agreed on was the well-being of Alexis.

One day, while Madison was picking Alexis up from daycare, she saw her mother's sister Keisha. Keisha asked Madison when she would be starting school. At first Madison was offended with her aunt for intruding in her business, but later, she'd apologized to her because she knew that her aunt was only looking out for her welfare.

Keisha: Madison, you remind me of myself when I was your age. I don't want you to wait as long as I did to finally go back to school. Go now while you have the support of your family.
Madison: I'll go, Auntie. I guess I'll go.
 Keisha: I know you will because I have already completed your financial aid and your

application for the community college.

Madison: Auntie, thanks a lot.

Madison was nervous about stepping back on a college campus again. This time, she was attending because she wanted to be at school, but the first time she attended college, she'd enrolled to make her family members happy. She did not know what she wanted to major in because she felt that she could do anything. She began to consider the things that she was good at in her attempts to choose a major. Madison enjoyed counseling her friends when they had problems, and she was a natural at it, but she also enjoyed mathematics. She weighed her options and decided that psychology would be her major.

****

Madison walked into class and saw a gentleman by the name of Ben, and Ben was very quiet and mild. He looked in her direction and asked about her day. Madison didn't know how to react. She had been praying and asking God to let her become friends with someone who would care about everything that concerned her. Hearing Ben specifically ask about her day made her want to get to know him better.

Madison and Ben exchanged numbers and almost immediately, they began to hang out. Their first date was in the workout room of the college. Ben asked Madison to hang out with him, and she suggested that they both workout together.

After playing basketball at the gym, the usher (a man from Madison's church) threw the basketball to her from across the room. Ben asked Madison if she knew the gentleman who'd thrown the ball, and Madison responded,

"Yes, I know, Mr. Joe. He goes to my church."

Ben then informed Madison that Mr. Joe was his father and Madison was shocked. This date was the beginning of many dates in the months to come. After enjoying romantic conversations and Ben's presence, Madison was floored by a revelation Ben revealed to her about his past. Ben was a Navy man who had traveled all over the world. He'd resided in Japan for some time where he had a girlfriend. According to Ben, now that he was back in the United States, thoughts of his girlfriend were mere fragments of his past.

One day, while Madison was at work, Ben came to Madison's job to inform her that his girlfriend had bought her ticket and would be in the States with him for two months.
In shock, Madison responded, "Okay," before walking away. Ben had made her feel alive,

and to receive such bad news tore her up inside.

Ben called Madison several times while his girlfriend was visiting him, but she told him not to contact her anymore and he agreed.

As time went by, Madison missed talking with her friend. At times, she'd get upset because she'd let her guards down.

Five years went by, and Madison and Ben barely said anything other than hello to each other. They frequented the same places; they attended the same church, the same university, and liked to hang out at the same night club. Although Madison did not allow Ben in her circle, she'd thought of him often. She would drive by his house hoping that he would be outside, but he never was. After a while, she rarely saw him at church, and because they had different majors, she rarely saw him at school.

Madison felt like every male she'd loved and cared for had found a way to exit her life. She was tired of being abandoned, so she decided to become celibate. She began refocusing her mind on continuing college, working, and raising her daughter. Alexis was her heart and joy. She didn't want Alexis to want or need for anything, so she decided to change her major from Psychology to Social Work. She wanted to be in a field that would allow her to serve families.

One Sunday morning, Ben was at church when he saw Madison. She looked as if she needed a friend. At that time, Jazzy was in the hospital and she was worried about her mother. Ben came over and encouraged her. He volunteered to go to the hospital with her. Ben was such a phenomenal help in that time that Madison could not imagine her life without him.

On February 2, 2009, Ben and Madison got married and added to their union was Mia and Shaun (Ben's children). The family now had a total of two girls and one son. Even though Madison was happy about all of the good things that were happening in her life, she still had a sadness and a void on the inside of her. She did not know what it was or even how to remove it. She needed help because something was missing.

Chapter 8

The Chance

One fall night, Madison woke up at two-thirty in the morning. She felt horrible, her heart was racing, and she startled Ben by jumping out of bed while holding her chest. Madison was so frightened that she did not wait for her husband to get dressed; instead, she drove herself and two of her children to the hospital.

Normally, the drive from Madison's home to the hospital was approximately seven minutes, but on that night, the drive to the hospital felt as if it were longer. With each second, Madison felt weaker and more desperate. She felt as if she was going to pass out.

Alexis was with her mother. Worried, she said, "Everything is going to be alright, Mom."

At the time, Madison wanted to believe her

daughter, but she had a little doubt.

Once at the hospital, Madison drove her car onto the ramp where the ambulances were stationed. A gray haired security guard ran out to meet the frantic Madison. The man asked Madison if everything was alright. She looked at him, and then, she looked at her daughters.

"Please take good care of them until my husband arrives," she said to the guard. It was at that moment that Madison knew that her life was not her own. She knew that she needed to truly trust in the God she had been told about. It was time to pray like never before. It was time to get for real about God.

A nurse dressed in blue scrubs called for Madison. She took Madison's vitals and performed an EKG, but the readings were not accurate and had the nurse baffled and Madison was afraid.

The Chance

Suddenly, a calmness came over her. In her heart, she heard, "I'll give you a peace that surpasses all understanding."

Madison knew she had heard this voice before when she was visiting church with her Uncle Kyle. She began to meditate on those words.

In the lobby of the hospital, Ben tried to keep the children calm. He prayed that God would allow his wife to pull through. Ben and the children needed Madison. She was his strength, his friend, and an awesome wife. The children prayed with their father that their mother was okay.

After being held for observation for several hours, Madison was released from the hospital. The doctor had scheduled her for an appointment with a cardiologist, and he'd also given her a heart monitor to wear for a few weeks.

The Chance

She had went to several doctor's appointments, and she started to have several episodes of racing and rapid heartbeats a day. Doctors could not explain her symptoms.

One morning, Madison was feeling sick, so she asked her sister, Mallory, to pray with her. She asked God to reassure her that she would be around to raise her three beautiful children. Madison knew that her family and her husband would provide for the children if something were to happen to her. Nevertheless, she wanted to see her children graduate and have children of their own, and she wanted to see this while she was in good health. The sisters cried out to the Lord with hopes that He heard every prayer that was sent out.

The following day, Mallory wanted to go to the mall to buy a shirt, and she'd asked Madison to travel with her because she did not want to leave her sister alone. Madison agreed and the two went to the mall.

While walking down the aisle of one of the stores in the mall, Madison's phone rang. Madison did not want to answer the phone so Mallory answered it for her while she sat down on a bench nearby. It was a call from Madison's cardiologist. This alarmed them both because it was Tuesday, and Madison wasn't scheduled to go back to the doctor until Thursday. The doctor asked if he could speak with Madison.

When Madison got the phone, the doctor asked her if she was sitting down because he had news for her. The doctor's office had canceled Madison's Thursday appointment, and the reason, as it turned out was: Madison was pregnant.

After hanging up the line, Mallory called

everyone she knew because she was in shock. She was not shocked at the news, but she was in awe of how God cared enough about her to send a precious life as a reassurance that she would remain on earth to raise her own children.

The scales fell from Madison's eyes that day. Madison had searched for happiness through people and through things, but that void had never been filled. It was that day that she began to praise God for allowing her to see Him as God of a second chance, God of life, God of creation, and God of the universe. In Madison's life, God had just shown her that He was the missing peace.